Environment *in Focus*

Greenhouse Gases

Cheryl Jakab

Marshall Cavendish
Benchmark
New York

This edition first published in 2011 in the United States of America by
Marshall Cavendish Benchmark
An imprint of Marshall Cavendish Corporation

Website: www.marshallcavendish.us

This publication represents the opinions and views of the author based on Cheryl Jakab's personal experience, knowledge, and research. The information in this book serves as a general guide only. The author and publisher have used their best efforts in preparing this book and disclaim liability rising directly and indirectly from the use and application of this book.

Other Marshall Cavendish Offices:
Marshall Cavendish International (Asia) Private Limited, 1 New Industrial Road, Singapore 536196 • Marshall Cavendish International (Thailand) Co Ltd. 253 Asoke, 12th Flr, Sukhumvit 21 Road, Klongtoey Nua, Wattana, Bangkok 10110, Thailand • Marshall Cavendish (Malaysia) Sdn Bhd, Times Subang, Lot 46, Subang Hi-Tech Industrial Park, Batu Tiga, 40000 Shah Alam, Selangor Darul Ehsan, Malaysia

Marshall Cavendish is a trademark of Times Publishing Limited

All websites were available and accurate when this book was sent to press.

Library of Congress Cataloging-in-Publication Data

Jakab, Cheryl.
  Greenhouse gases / Cheryl Jakab.
    p. cm. — (Environment in focus)
  Summary: "Discusses the environmental issue of greenhouse gases and how to create a sustainable way of living"—Provided by publisher.
  Includes bibliographical references and index.
  ISBN 978-1-60870-091-2
  1. Greenhouse gases—Environmental aspects—Juvenile literature. 2. Pollution—Juvenile literature. I. Title.
  TD885.5.G73J35 2011
  363.738'74—dc22
                    2009042319

First published in 2010 by
MACMILLAN EDUCATION AUSTRALIA PTY LTD
15–19 Claremont Street, South Yarra 3141

Visit our website at www.macmillan.com.au or go directly to www.macmillanlibrary.com.au

Associated companies and representatives throughout the world.

Edited by Margaret Maher
Text and cover design by Cristina Neri, Canary Graphic Design
Page layout by Domenic Lauricella
Photo research by Sarah Johnson
Illustration on p. 5 by Richard Morden. Other illustrations by Domenic Lauricella
Maps courtesy of Geo Atlas

Printed in the United States

Acknowledgments
The author and the publisher are grateful to the following for permission to reproduce copyright material:

Front cover photograph: blue sky and exhaust smoke, © joyfull/Shutterstock

© Anna Clopet/CORBIS, 22; © Bob Daemmrich/CORBIS, 14; © Toru Yamanaka/Pool/epa/CORBIS, 26; Mark Fergus/CSIRO, 15; Paul Kane/ Stringer/Getty Images, 27; © charliebishop/iStockphoto, 7 (bottom), 21; © gniedzieska/iStockphoto, 20; © Scott Indermaur /Jupiter Images, 23; Image copyright © Commander John Bortniak, NOAA Corps (ret.), 6 (bottom left), 13; Image copyright © NOAA George E. Marsh Album, 6 (bottom right), 9; Photolibrary/Sue Darlow, 19; Peter Harrison/Photolibrary, 25; Cape Grim BAPS/Fraser/SPL/Photolibrary, 18; Cordelia Molloy/SPL/Photolibrary, 28; Chevalier Virginie/Photolibrary, 29; Dr. Vladimir Romanovsky, University of Alaska Fairbanks, 7 (top), 17; © R. Marion /Shutterstock, 8; © Pinosub/ Shutterstock, 10; © Viorel Sima/Shutterstock, 16; © Michel Stevelmans/Shutterstock, 7 (middle), 24; © Mark William Richardson/Shutterstock, 11.

While every care has been taken to trace and acknowledge copyright, the publisher tenders their apologies for any accidental infringement where copyright has proved untraceable. Where the attempt has been unsuccessful, the publisher welcomes information that would redress the situation.

Please note
At the time of printing, the Internet addresses appearing in this book were correct. Owing to the dynamic nature of the Internet, however, we cannot guarantee that all these addresses will remain correct.

Contents

Glossary Words
When a word is printed in **bold**, you can look up its meaning in the Glossary on page 31.

Environment in Focus

Hi there! This is Earth speaking. Will you spare a moment to listen to me? I have some very important things to discuss.

We must focus on some urgent environmental problems! All living things depend on my environment, but the way you humans are living at the moment, I will not be able to keep looking after you.

The issues I am worried about are:
- large ecological footprints
- damage to natural wonders
- widespread pollution in the environment
- the release of **greenhouse gases** into the **atmosphere**
- poor management of waste
- environmental damage caused by food production

My challenge to you is to find a **sustainable** way of living. Read on to find out what people around the world are doing to try to help.

Fast Fact
Concerned people in local, national, and international groups are trying to understand how our way of life causes environmental problems. This important work helps us learn how to live more sustainably now and in the future.

What's the Issue?
Increasing Greenhouse Gases

Greenhouse gases in the atmosphere are increasing rapidly. These gases cause **global warming** by contributing to the greenhouse effect.

The Natural Greenhouse Effect

Greenhouse gases, such as **carbon dioxide** and water vapor, help keep Earth warm. The gases act like the walls of a greenhouse, which keep the inside warmer than the outside. Without this natural greenhouse effect Earth's surface would be about 68 degrees cooler than it is today.

Adding to the Natural Greenhouse Effect

Many activities, particularly burning coal and other **fossil fuels**, emit greenhouse gases. When these greenhouse gases reach the upper layers of the atmosphere they add to the natural greenhouse effect. This causes Earth's average temperature to rise.

Fast Fact
Earth's average temperature could increase by more than 39 °Fahrenheit (4 °Celsius) by 2100 if greenhouse gas **emissions** are not reduced.

Greenhouse gases in Earth's atmosphere trap warmth from the Sun, creating the natural greenhouse effect.

Greenhouse gases

Greenhouse Gas Issues

The most urgent greenhouse gas issues around the globe include:

- acceptance of the fact that greenhouse gases lead to global warming
- increasing amounts of carbon dioxide in the atmosphere
- increasing levels of **methane** in the atmosphere
- identifying sources of **nitrous oxide**
- the need to reduce per-person greenhouse gas emissions

NORTH AMERICA

United States

NORTH ATLANTIC OCEAN

Hawaii

Equator

SOUTH AMERICA

ISSUE 1

United States
Early investigations of the greenhouse effect were undertaken after the Dust Bowl in the 1930s. See pages 8–11.

ISSUE 2

Hawaii
Measurements taken in Hawaii show rising levels of carbon dioxide. See pages 12–15.

Around the Globe

ISSUE 3

Arctic Circle
Permafrost that is melting due to global warming is releasing methane, a greenhouse gas. See pages 16–19.

Arctic Circle

EUROPE

ASIA

AFRICA

ISSUE 5

Australia
Australia has high greenhouse gas emissions per person. See pages 24–27.

INDIAN

OCEAN

AUSTRALIA

ISSUE 4

Europe
Use of **fertilizers** is increasing the amount of nitrous oxide in the atmosphere. See pages 20–23.

Fast Fact
Greenhouse gases make up only a very small part of Earth's atmosphere (less than one percent). The other 99 percent is made up of about 78 percent **nitrogen** and 21 percent oxygen.

Accepting the Greenhouse Problem

There is a lot of evidence that connects the rise in greenhouse gases to human activity. However, many people still do not accept that there is a problem.

The Increased Greenhouse Effect

The increased greenhouse effect was demonstrated by Svante Arrhenius, a Swedish scientist, in 1896. He showed that Earth's average temperature would rise if the amounts of different gases in the atmosphere changed. Arrhenius was the first to suggest that burning fossil fuels would increase the greenhouse effect.

Rising Temperatures

Recorded temperatures between 1900 and 2000 rose by an average of about 33 degrees Fahrenheit (0.6 °C). However, many people still argue that Earth is not warming, or that the warming is not due to people's activities. Most scientists agree that the evidence shows that Earth is warming. They believe the most likely cause is human activity.

Rising temperatures have caused changes on Earth, such as melting of ice in polar regions.

Fast Fact
Arrhenius calculated that doubling the amount of carbon dioxide in the atmosphere would increase temperatures by 33 °Fahrenheit (0.6 °C).

Land clearing and plowing are now considered to have been the main causes of the dust storms in the Dust Bowl.

CASE STUDY
Early Evidence of Global Warming

The disaster known as the Dust Bowl occurred in the 1930s in the midwestern United States. It led many people to wonder if Earth was getting warmer.

The Dust Bowl

The Dust Bowl was one of the worst environmental disasters of the 1900s. Drought and dust storms forced about 3 million people to leave farms in the Great Plains. The plains were experiencing higher than normal temperatures and reduced rainfall.

Recorded Warming

In the 1930s, reports of warmer temperatures became common. An English engineer named Guy Stewart Callendar decided to examine weather records from across the world. He found that between 1890 and 1935 temperatures had warmed by 33 degrees Fahrenheit (0.6 °C).

Fast Fact
Climate modeling shows that there will be more extreme weather as Earth warms. This could include more frequent and severe hurricanes, more heat waves, and more tornadoes.

Toward a Sustainable Future: Reducing Greenhouse Gases

Today the evidence shows that **climate change** is happening. The need to reduce greenhouse gas emissions is urgent. These reductions are being achieved through international agreements.

International Agreements

The first international agreement on climate change, the Kyoto Protocol, was adopted in 1997. It established limits on greenhouse gas emissions from fossil fuels and other **pollutants**. At a meeting in Bali in 2007, countries agreed on new targets for reducing greenhouse gases. These will come into effect in 2012.

Climate Skeptics

Fast Fact
The IPCC is a group of experts who provide reports on climate science. These reports are based on the work of thousands of scientists to provide the best information possible.

Despite the evidence, there are still people who argue that global warming is not really happening. These people are sometimes called "climate change deniers" or "climate skeptics." In 2007 the Intergovernmental Panel on Climate Change (IPCC) reported that it is "clear beyond doubt that climate change is a reality."

Using renewable energy, such as electricity generated by solar panels, can help reduce greenhouse gas emissions.

Coal-fired power stations emit water vapor as well as large amounts of carbon dioxide.

CASE STUDY
The Kyoto Protocol

The United Nations Kyoto Protocol of 1997 was the first international agreement that set target levels for greenhouse gas emissions.

The Greenhouse Gases

The Kyoto Protocol targets were set by the IPCC. They limit **developed countries'** emissions of six greenhouse gases until 2012. These greenhouse gases are:

- carbon dioxide
- methane
- nitrous oxide
- chlorofluorocarbons (CFCs)
- hydrofluorocarbons
- tetrafluoromethane

Long-Term Targets

The long-term aim of the Kyoto Protocol is to bring world emissions to half the 1990 levels by 2050. Eventually, total greenhouse gas emissions need to be less than 10 **gigatons**.

Fast Fact

Water vapor also adds to the greenhouse effect, but the amounts in the atmosphere depend on temperature and climate. People cannot directly change these amounts to tackle global warming.

The Increase in Carbon Dioxide

Carbon dioxide is the main greenhouse gas that is increasing due to human activity. This gas is also known by its **chemical symbol**, CO_2.

Sources of Carbon Dioxide

Many of our activities use fossil fuels and produce carbon dioxide. This includes using electricity from coal-fired power stations, traveling in cars and planes, growing food, and manufacturing goods. Today, more than three-quarters of people's carbon dioxide emissions come from burning coal, oil, and gas. Some of this carbon dioxide will stay in the air for centuries or even longer.

Fast Fact

In 2008, the level of carbon dioxide in the atmosphere rose to 385 parts per million. This was more than at any other time in the last 650,000 years.

Carbon Dioxide in the Atmosphere

The amount of carbon dioxide in the atmosphere can be measured in parts per million. Carbon dioxide levels are now one hundred parts per million higher than at the beginning of the 1800s. These levels continue to rise.

The amount of carbon dioxide in the atmosphere has risen sharply in the last fifty years.

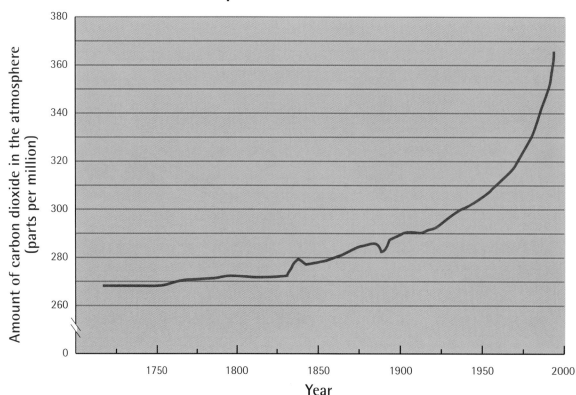

The Increase of Carbon Dioxide in the Atmosphere Between 1750 and 2000

Amount of carbon dioxide in the atmosphere (parts per million)

Year

The Mauna Loa Observatory, which monitors carbon dioxide levels in the atmosphere, is on the Mauna Loa volcano in Hawaii.

CASE STUDY

Carbon Dioxide Monitoring

The first long-term carbon dioxide monitoring station was established at an observatory on Mauna Loa, a volcano in Hawaii. Measurements from this observatory began in 1957 and continue to this day.

The Monitoring Program

Charles David Keeling directed the Mauna Loa monitoring program. Keeling wanted to find out whether carbon dioxide levels really were rising. To do this, he planned to take measurements over many years.

The Keeling Curve

In 1960, Keeling reported the results of the monitoring program using the "Keeling curve." This graph showed that carbon dioxide levels were rising much earlier than anyone expected.

Since 2000, annual carbon dioxide increases of two parts per million or more have been common. This is compared to 1.5 parts per million in the 1980s and less than one part per million during the 1960s.

Fast Fact
Carbon dioxide levels go up and down during each year. This is because plants absorb different amounts of carbon dioxide throughout the year, depending on the temperature.

13

Toward a Sustainable Future: Reducing Carbon Dioxide Emissions

Reducing carbon dioxide emissions is vital for a sustainable future. There are many changes that can be made to reduce emissions.

Ways To Reduce Emissions

Changes that will help reduce overall emissions include:

- replacing fossil fuel power sources with renewable alternatives, such as solar, wind, and wave power
- increasing the energy efficiency of appliances
- designing more energy-efficient transportation systems
- reducing emissions from fossil fuels, such as by using **carbon sequestration** to store emissions from burning coal

Carbon Sinks

Fast Fact

Fossil fuels are ancient carbon sinks that have held carbon underground. This carbon was absorbed by plants in forests that grew millions of years ago.

Plants can be used as carbon sinks. This means they can be used to store carbon dioxide. Plants take in carbon dioxide from the atmosphere when they grow. They hold that carbon until they die and decay. Planting trees is therefore another way to reduce carbon dioxide levels in the atmosphere.

New forms of transportation, such as solar-powered cars, are being developed to help reduce carbon dioxide emissions.

HySSIL concrete weighs only half as much as normal concrete, so it requires less energy for transportation.

CASE STUDY

Developing "Greener" Concrete

Concrete production is one of the major sources of greenhouse gas emissions. It generates about 7 to 10 percent of emissions worldwide. This is due to the huge amount of concrete that is produced. It is also due to the very high temperatures used in its making.

A New Form of Concrete

In 2005, a research organization in Australia announced a new form of concrete, called HySSIL. It is as strong as normal concrete but is much lighter. It has better **insulation** than normal concrete and is strong and fire resistant. Because of this, it will increase the energy efficiency of concrete buildings.

HySSIL is also easily **recyclable**. Because it is lightweight, it will lead to reduced greenhouse gas emissions. This is because less energy will be needed to transport the concrete and use it in construction.

Fast Fact
Many **developing countries** have rapidly increasing greenhouse gas emissions as building increases and industry develops.

The Increase in Methane

Methane is the second most powerful greenhouse gas from human sources. Rising levels of methane may be responsible for 20 percent of today's greenhouse effect.

How Methane Forms

Methane forms when material from living things decays underwater. It also forms in the stomachs and intestines of some animals, particularly cows, sheep, buffalo, and termites. Livestock farming, rice growing, and mining of fossil fuels are all human activities that add methane to the atmosphere.

Levels of Methane

Fast Fact
Permanently irrigated rice paddies in Asia emit large amounts of methane into the atmosphere.

Since 1750, levels of methane in the atmosphere have more than doubled. They may double again by 2050. Each year about 315 to 440 million tons of methane are released into the air.

Methane stays in the atmosphere for only about ten to twelve years. However, it has a major warming effect. It traps twenty to twenty-five times more heat than carbon dioxide.

Increasing numbers of livestock, such as cows, are adding to methane emissions.

This sinkhole near Fairbanks, Alaska, formed due to the melting of a large ice pocket within permafrost.

CASE STUDY
Melting Permafrost in the Arctic Circle

In 2007, methane levels were found to be rising for the first time since 1998. The explanation for this may be the melting of permafrost in the Arctic Circle.

Permafrost

Permafrost is permanently frozen ground. About a quarter of the soil in the Northern Hemisphere is permafrost. In the past, the top layer of this soil melted in the summer, then refroze each year. Today, soil layers across the Arctic Circle are melting and not freezing again.

Fast Fact
The amount of methane produced by farm animals increases when they are fed a rich diet.

Methane Release

Scientists are concerned that the Arctic Circle will continue to warm and more permafrost will thaw. This would allow bacteria to feed on the carbon in the soils. As they feed, these bacteria release large amounts of methane.

Toward a Sustainable Future: Monitoring Methane Levels

It is difficult to predict how long methane levels will increase in the atmosphere. This will depend on farming methods and the melting of ice at Earth's poles. Monitoring sources and levels of methane is vital. This will help scientists develop ways of dealing with methane emissions in the future.

Reduced Methane in the Atmosphere

The amount of methane in the atmosphere leveled out in the late 1990s. This may have been due to better management of rice irrigation and mining exploration, and better processing of fossil fuels. More methane was captured from trash dumps, which also reduced the amount of methane released into the atmosphere.

Monitoring Emissions

The World Data Center for Greenhouse Gases in Japan monitors all greenhouse gas emissions. It files and distributes atmospheric observations from forty-four different meteorological organizations.

Fast Fact
Information about current levels of greenhouse gases is published in the Greenhouse Gas Bulletin.

The Cape Grim monitoring station in Tasmania, Australia, is one of the stations that monitor methane emissions.

Dryland rice can be grown without flooding, so it does not add to methane emissions.

CASE STUDY

Changing Ways of Growing Rice

New rice-growing techniques in China are reducing the methane produced by this important food crop.

Methane from Rice Growing

About 18 percent of the methane produced by humans is from rice growing. Bacteria in the wet soils of irrigated rice paddies release methane into the atmosphere.

Changing Rice Growing

Changing methods of rice growing can reduce methane emissions by more than one-third. Many Chinese farmers are now using **crop rotation** and drain fields several times a year instead of keeping them flooded. Farmers can also plant rice varieties that can be grown without flooding. This change in rice growing may have slowed the increase of methane in the atmosphere over the last twenty years.

Fast Fact

The amount of methane produced by cows is affected by what they eat. For example, cows digest some plants more easily than others. Eating these plants reduces the methane the cows produce.

Nitrous Oxide

Nitrous oxide is the next most powerful greenhouse gas after carbon dioxide and methane. It is more than three hundred times as effective as carbon dioxide at trapping heat. However, there are much lower levels of nitrous oxide in the atmosphere.

Sources of Nitrous Oxide

Sources of nitrous oxide include tiny organisms in soil and oceans, as well as human activities. The main way humans add nitrous oxide to the atmosphere is by using fertilizers that contain nitrogen. Burning fossil fuels, burning wood, and treating human waste also release nitrous oxide.

Fast Fact
The other three main greenhouse gases are called CFC-11, CFC-12 and CFC-113. These gases are produced from human activity, with no known natural sources.

Nitrous Oxide in the Atmosphere

Nitrous oxide makes up only a very small part of the atmosphere. However, it can remain in the atmosphere for up to 150 years. Nitrous oxide released today will add to the greenhouse effect well into the future.

Burning wood, such as for a fire, releases small amounts of nitrous oxide.

Many farmers in Europe spray their crops with industrial nitrogen fertilizers.

CASE STUDY
Dependence on Nitrogen Fertilizers

European agriculture is very dependent on nitrogen fertilizers made by industrial processes. However, there are several problems associated with using these fertilizers. These include the amount of energy needed to make the fertilizers and the nitrous oxide emissions they can cause.

Consumption of Nitrogen Fertilizer

The global consumption of nitrogen fertilizer is about 80 million tons per year. The amount of nitrogen estimated to be added to soil naturally by living things is 110 to 130 million tons.

Greenhouse Gases and Fertilizer

Much of the nitrogen from fertilizers applied to farmland is absorbed into the plants that grow there. However, the nitrogen is not always completely absorbed. The leftover nitrogen is released into the atmosphere as ammonia or nitrous oxide. This adds to the greenhouse effect.

Fast Fact

Ammonia, which contains nitrogen, is a substance used in making fertilizer. Today, the production of ammonia consumes about 5 percent of natural gas across the globe.

Toward a Sustainable Future: Reducing Nitrous Oxide

Nitrous oxide is a significant contributor to global warming. It is an urgent problem that needs to be addressed.

Nitrogen Fixing

Peas, beans, and other **legumes** naturally fix nitrogen. This means they take nitrogen from the air and add it to soil. Using these plants to add nitrogen to soil generates less nitrous oxide than using industrial fertilizer. Increasing the use of legume crops in agriculture could reduce the amount of nitrous oxide produced.

Making Soil Fertile

Fertilizers are added to soil to provide nutrients for crop plants. However, there are other ways to do this. This includes adding mulch, fresh green plant material, and naturally decomposed plant materials to soil. This improves soil fertility while reducing the need for industrially produced nitrogen fertilizer.

Fast Fact
Two new gases called nitrogen trifluoride and sulfuryl fluoride have recently been found to be increasing in the atmosphere. These gases also add to the greenhouse effect.

Compost, or decomposed plant material, can be added to soil to provide nutrients.

Legumes, such as soya beans, can be grown to put nitrogen into soil.

CASE STUDY
Nitrogen and Legume Crops

Legumes such as peas, chickpeas, and lentils can take nitrogen from the atmosphere and convert it into a form plants can use.

How Can Legumes Reduce Nitrous Oxide?

Legume plants have nitrogen-fixing bacteria in their roots. They can be used to add nitrogen to the soil instead of adding industrial nitrogen fertilizer. Any nitrogen fixed by the crop and not removed at harvest of the plant remains in the soil. This means it is available for the following crop.

Sustainable Fertilizer

Using legumes is a sustainable way of adding nitrogen to soil. Before the use of industrial nitrogen fertilizers became common, agricultural systems included a legume crop to fix nitrogen in the soil. One way of doing this is to use crop rotation. For example, farmers can grow a pea crop followed by a crop that needs lots of nitrogen in soil.

High Greenhouse Gas Emissions Per Person

In 2009, evidence showed that global warming is happening more quickly than predicted. However, greenhouse gas emissions per person are still high in many countries. Even if emission levels set by international agreements are reached, reversing climate change will be slow.

Exceeding Targets

Developed countries are exceeding the greenhouse gas emission targets developed under the Kyoto Accords. Carbon dioxide emissions were higher in 2000 than they were in 1990, and they are still rising. Although reductions of some gases have been achieved, current emissions per person worldwide are three times what they would need to be to reduce greenhouse gases to 1990 levels. Emissions are still rising in most countries.

Many people in developed countries use cars for transportation, adding to greenhouse gas emissions.

Fast Fact
In 1990, total human greenhouse gas emissions were estimated to be about 41 gigatons. In 2005, the total emissions were approximately 45 gigatons. By 2030 the amount is predicted to be 42 gigatons.

24

Australia produces large amounts of coal, which it uses in coal-fired power stations to produce electricity.

CASE STUDY

High Greenhouse Gas Emissions in Australia

Australia is a developed country with a small total population. However, on average, Australians emit more greenhouse gas per person than any other country.

Coal-Fired Power Stations

Part of the reason for Australia's high emissions is its use of coal-fired power stations to generate electricity. Burning coal releases huge amounts of greenhouse gases into the atmosphere.

Reducing Emissions

Many individuals, groups, governments, and companies across Australia show great concern about the level of emissions. A number of people are changing to renewable energy sources, such as solar energy, to reduce emissions. Some reductions are also being achieved by planting trees to offset, or absorb, emissions. In late 2007 Australia finally signed the Kyoto Protocol after a change of government. However, Australia still has a large **carbon footprint**.

Fast Fact

In 2006, the countries with the highest greenhouse gas emissions per person were:
1. Australia
2. United States
3. Canada
4. Saudi Arabia
5. Russia

Toward a Sustainable Future: Urgent Greenhouse Gas Action

All countries need to reduce greenhouse gas emissions to avoid problems for future generations. Today, most people understand that urgent action is needed.

The Timeline

The necessary timeline for reducing greenhouse gases is now clear. To reach the global target, emissions must be halved by the middle of the twenty-first century. To achieve this, average emissions will need to be about 2 tons (2 t) per person per year.

Greenhouse Gas Targets

Greenhouse gas emissions targets must be set according to effectiveness, efficiency, and equity. Any future changes to targets need to be effective in preventing climate change. They must also make the use of fuels more efficient to conserve resources. Finally, emissions targets need to be fair to all countries.

Fast Fact

Under the Kyoto Protocol, developed countries can help meet their emissions targets by paying for emissions cuts in other countries. For example, a developed country could invest in wind farms in a developing country.

Politicians from countries around the world attend meetings to set greenhouse gas targets.

H₂ Fuel Cell Bus

Cott CAT

Businesses can reduce emissions by developing new technologies, such as vehicles that do not produce greenhouse gases.

CASE STUDY
The Australian Emissions Trading Plan

The Australian government is planning to put in place a greenhouse gas **emissions trading plan**.

Emissions Trading Plans

Countries set up emissions trading plans to help meet emissions targets. "Cap and trade" plans are the most widely used. A cap, or upper limit, is placed on business greenhouse gas emissions. The government gives businesses permits to emit greenhouse gases up to the cap. Businesses can trade emissions permits. This allows them to find the cheapest way to meet their emissions targets.

The Australian Plan

The Australian plan will include laws to make it compulsory to report emissions of the six greenhouse gases named in the Kyoto Protocol. The laws cover emissions from companies involved in energy production or supply, industry, and waste treatment.

What Can You Do? Reduce Your Greenhouse Gas Emissions

Each individual's actions are important in reducing greenhouse gas emissions, as all the little savings add up.

Cut Down Your Emissions

You can cut down your emissions by making choices each day. For example, you can:

- turn off electrical appliances when you are not using them
- walk or ride a bike instead of driving, when possible
- use an extra blanket or quilt instead of an electric blanket on cold nights

Use Appliances Powered by Renewable Energy

Electrical appliances use energy. When the electricity supply comes from coal, they add to greenhouse gas emissions. Today, you can choose electrical appliances that use more environmentally friendly energy sources. These include wind-up radios and solar-powered flashlights.

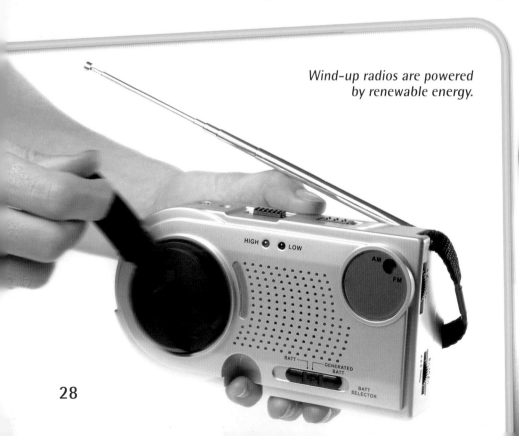

Wind-up radios are powered by renewable energy.

Fast Fact
The One Laptop per Child program aims to distribute computers to children in developing countries. The program has developed a wind-up minicomputer that costs less than $100.

Walking to school instead of going by car can reduce greenhouse gas emissions.

Use a Greenhouse Gas Emissions Calculator

Have you ever wanted to know what effect you have on greenhouse gas emissions in your home? You can find out by using one of the many online calculators.

Figure Out Your Emissions

Knowing how much greenhouse gas you are emitting allows you to figure out where you can make savings. Some calculators will compare your emissions with those of a typical house and those of an energy-efficient house. This comparison can give you ideas for ways to reduce your own greenhouse gas emissions.

Make Improvements

The next step is to put these ideas into action and make improvements. Every person on Earth must think about the greenhouses gases they produce and try to find ways to reduce them.

Toward a Sustainable Future

Well, I hope you now see that if you take up my challenge your world will be a better place. There are many ways to work toward a sustainable future. Imagine a world with:

- a sustainable ecological footprint
- places of natural heritage protected for the future
- no more environmental pollution
- less greenhouse gas in the air, reducing global warming
- zero waste and efficient use of resources
- a secure food supply for all

This is what you can achieve if you work together with my natural systems.

We must work together to live sustainably. That will mean a better environment and a better life for all living things on Earth, now and in the future.

Websites

For further information on greenhouse gases, visit the following websites.

- Environmental Kids Club www.epa.gov/kids/
- Marian Koshland Science Museum of the National Academy of Sciences www.koshland-science-museum.org/exhibitgcc/causes02.jsp
- National Geographic: Earth's Changing Climate http://ngm.nationalgeographic.com/climateconnections/climate-map

Glossary

atmosphere
The layers of gases surrounding Earth.

carbon dioxide
A colorless, odorless gas.

carbon footprint
The part of an ecological footprint that is due to carbon dioxide emissions.

carbon sequestration
Removing carbon dioxide from the air and pumping it underground to be stored.

chemical symbol
Letters and numbers that represent the chemicals a substance is made of.

climate change
Changes to the usual weather patterns in an area.

climate modeling
Scientific prediction of climate patterns.

crop rotation
Growing different crops in an area each season.

developed countries
Countries with industrial development, a strong economy, and a high standard of living.

developing countries
Countries with less developed industry, a poor economy, and a lower standard of living.

emissions
Substances released into the environment.

emissions trading plan
A system of trading that sells permits allowing people to emit certain amounts of greenhouse gases.

fertilizers
Substances added to soil that contain nutrients necessary for plant growth.

fossil fuels
Fuels such as oil, coal, and gas, that formed under the ground from the remains of animals and plants that lived millions of years ago.

gigatons
A thousand million tons (1,000,000,000 tons).

global warming
An increase in the average temperature on Earth.

greenhouse gases
Gases that help trap heat in Earth's atmosphere.

insulation
Material that prevents the transfer of heat and other forms of energy.

legumes
A group of plants which grow seeds inside a pod and naturally add nitrogen to soil.

methane
A gas that is given off from burning fossil fuels and decomposing vegetation, including the digestion of plants by animals.

nitrogen
A gas that makes up a large part of the atmosphere.

nitrous oxide
A long-lasting greenhouse gas that is produced mainly by the use of nitrogen fertilizers.

permafrost
Permanently frozen ground.

pollutants
Any unwanted substances in the environment.

recyclable
Able to be reprocessed so that it can be used again.

sustainable
Does not use more resources than Earth can regenerate.

Index